THE PAIL OF NAILS

Harriet May Savitz &
K. Michael Syring

Illustrated by Charles Shaw

ABINGDON PRESS

NASHVILLE

Library of Congress Cataloging-in-Publication Data

Savitz, Harriet May.
   The pail of nails / Harriet May Savitz, K. Michael Syring.
      p. cm.
   Summary: During a parade in Jerusalem, Marcus is asked by soldiers to carry a pail of nails to aid them in nailing to a cross a man whom Marcus recognizes as a kind and peaceable fisherman who is his friend.
ISBN 0-687-29974-8 (alk. paper)

   1. Jesus Christ—Crucifixion—Juvenile fiction. [1. Jesus Christ—Crucifixion—Fiction.]   I. Syring, K. Michael.   II. Title.
PZ7.S2664Pai   1989
[E]—dc19   88-7653
                                                                                                 CIP
                                                                                                  AC

Manufactured in Hong Kong

This book is dedicated to my family
—Leslie, Scott, Gretchen, and Jon—
who have filled my life with joy.

—K. M. S.

Marcus lived by the Sea of Galilee. He didn't have a father. His father had been a soldier in a forgotten war, and he had never returned.

Marcus walked on the sand by the Sea of Galilee. He walked alone. He thought of many things.

He thought of war. He thought of his father whom he would never see again. He thought of his mother who cried a lot at night. Marcus knew why she cried, but he couldn't help her.

While he sat on the beach by the sea, Marcus liked to watch the fishermen work on their nets before they went fishing for the day. Marcus wanted to be a fisherman. He wanted a boat of his own. He wanted his own nets. He wanted to bring his own prizes back from the sea.

One morning a man walked down the beach. He walked toward Marcus and smiled. The man's smile made Marcus want to smile back, and he did. Marcus thought the man must be a fisherman, for he seemed to be such a good friend to the fishermen whose boats went out to sea each day.

"Is it a good fishing day?" Marcus finally asked.

The man sat down next to him. "No," he shook his head, "but it is a good day anyway."

They became friends that day. They talked about fishing. Marcus liked that. He didn't have a father to talk to about things like fishing. They talked about boats. Marcus liked that too. And his new friend told stories. He told stories about people loving one another. It filled Marcus with a warm feeling. He wished he had a story to tell.

The fisherman was a gentle man. He told Marcus he had never been to war. He told Marcus that his father had told him that war was bad. Marcus understood. He didn't like killing either. Most boys his age took pride in wrestling, in fighting, in being the strongest of the strong. Marcus wasn't like them.

Marcus and the man met many times after that. They met when the sky was dark with clouds, and rain threatened the Sea of Galilee. They met when the wind whipped the sand and mixed it with the sea. The man said to Marcus, "Someday you will have your boat, if you really work for it and if you keep love in your heart."

This man had many friends. They talked, ran, and laughed together on the beach. Marcus laughed too. They played ball together. Marcus didn't feel alone anymore.

One day Marcus went to the beach as usual, but as soon as he stepped on the sand, he knew something was wrong. There were no boats on the Sea of Galilee. He looked as far up and down the beach as he could see. None of his friends was there. And his best friend, the fisherman, was gone too.

He went back to the beach the next day and the next. Still the beach was empty. There was no one to laugh with. There was no one to play ball with. Marcus wondered where his friend had gone. Why had he left without saying good-bye?

The next day his mother received a message. It came from Marcus's uncle in Jerusalem. There was trouble in the land. Small wars were breaking out everywhere.

"Come stay with me for a while," the uncle wrote. "You and Marcus will be safe here."

Marcus's mother decided to go.

Marcus said good-bye to the Sea of Galilee. He felt sure that he would never again see his friend the fisherman.

It took about five days for Marcus and his mother to travel to Jerusalem. They passed the town of Cana. Marcus remembered his friend had said he went there once. Could he be in Cana now? The desert air was hot. Marcus missed the breezes of the Sea of Galilee.

Jerusalem was a big city, the biggest Marcus had ever seen. From a distance, the buildings looked like towers of gold. The streets were filled with soldiers, and excitement was everywhere. It was Passover, the Jewish holiday. Even the governor was there. People were coming to Jerusalem from all over the country.

Marcus and his mother settled at his uncle's house. And then his uncle said, "Come, let us go and watch the festivities."

They went to the center of the city. Marcus had never seen so many people gathered in one place before. He was surprised when a soldier marching in the parade grabbed him by the hand and pulled him into the line. His mother didn't have a chance to say anything.

And then the soldier beside him said, "Here, boy, carry this pail of nails for me. I have carried it long enough."

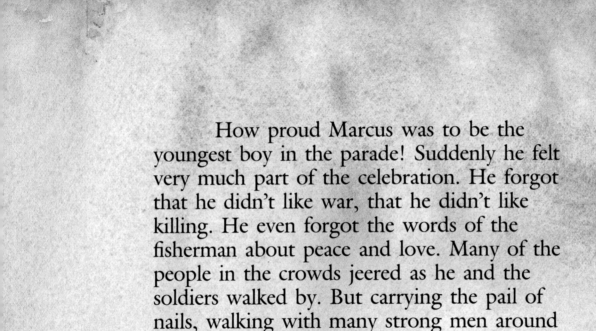

How proud Marcus was to be the youngest boy in the parade! Suddenly he felt very much part of the celebration. He forgot that he didn't like war, that he didn't like killing. He even forgot the words of the fisherman about peace and love. Many of the people in the crowds jeered as he and the soldiers walked by. But carrying the pail of nails, walking with many strong men around him, Marcus wasn't afraid.

So Marcus found himself in his first parade, laughing with many of the soldiers, walking along proudly with his mother and uncle watching and waving.

They walked through the town, then out of Jerusalem.

Suddenly the parade stopped. Marcus heard someone call out, "Where is the boy with the pail of nails?"

Marcus stepped forward quickly. He walked past the soldiers to the head of the parade. And then he was there in front of the long line of soldiers, in front of all the people who had run in the streets along the sides of the parade. He held the pail of nails, but he could not speak. Marcus just stood there, his eyes open wide, not believing what he saw in front of him.

There, lying on the ground, was his fisherman friend, who looked at him with understanding in his eyes. Someone took the pail of nails from Marcus. Someone took his fisherman friend and nailed him to a cross.

Marcus looked around. Why didn't someone help his friend? Why didn't someone speak up? Where were all the friends who had run and laughed on the beach? Were they too afraid to help him now? Was this a part of war? Why were the soldiers happy? What could his fisherman friend have done so wrong?

Marcus searched the crowd of faces for his mother and uncle. He could not see them.

So Marcus stood there in front of his friend on the cross, feeling the pain that his friend felt. He looked up at him, wanting to ask, Why? How? What for? But his friend looked down and shook his head as if to say, Don't speak.

Marcus just stood there in silence with the empty pail of nails at his feet. The people behind him began to leave. The sun slid slowly down behind the cross.

The sky grew dark, but still Marcus stood there.

His uncle said, "Come Marcus, it's time to go." But Marcus shook his head and explained that he must stay with his friend for a little while longer.

His uncle and his mother waited down the road.

Marcus's friend couldn't talk anymore. He wouldn't be able to tell anybody that war was bad, that love was good, and that all people were brothers and sisters. But then, why had they nailed him to the cross?

His mother came at last to get him. "Marcus," she asked as they walked away from the cross, "how did you know that man?"

Marcus didn't answer. The answers were deep in his heart. But as he walked down the road away from the cross, he knew what he would do.

Someday he would go back to the Sea of Galilee. Someday he would have his own boat, his own nets, his own prize from the sea. He would work toward that dream as his friend had told him to.

And wherever he went, he would remember the fisherman and tell his stories of love and peace. That way his friend would always be with him, and he would never be alone again.